Aussie CHOMPS

68 TEETH

It's the school holidays and Jack plans to fish. But he attracts something bigger than a barramundi: a croc has entered the river on his family's property and it's hungry!

It will make a great story, but will Jack survive to tell the tale?

Grab another Chomp!

Anton Rocks On!
David Metzenthen

Boots and All
Sherryl Clark

The Boy Who Would Live Forever
Moya Simons

Grommet Saves the World
James Moloney

The Really, Really High Diving Tower
David Metzenthen

Stella by the Sea
Ruth Starke

Walter Wants to be a Werewolf!
Richard Harland

I Hate Sport
Prue Storer

Aussie CHOMPS

68 Teeth

James Moloney

Puffin Books

For my nephew, Paul Moloney

PUFFIN BOOKS

Published by the Penguin Group
Penguin Group (Australia)
250 Camberwell Road, Camberwell, Victoria 3124, Australia
(a division of Pearson Australia Group Pty Ltd)
Penguin Group (USA) Inc.
375 Hudson Street, New York, New York 10014, USA
Penguin Group (Canada)
10 Alcorn Avenue, Toronto, Ontario, Canada, M4V 3B2
(a division of Pearson Penguin Canada Inc.)
Penguin Books Ltd
80 Strand, London WC2R 0RL, England
Penguin Ireland
25 St Stephen's Green, Dublin 2, Ireland
(a division of Penguin Books Ltd)
Penguin Books India Pvt Ltd
11, Community Centre, Panchsheel Park, New Delhi-110 017, India
Penguin Group (NZ)
Cnr Airborne and Rosedale Roads, Albany, Auckland, New Zealand
(a division of Pearson New Zealand Ltd)
Penguin Books (South Africa) (Pty) Ltd
24 Sturdee Avenue, Rosebank, Johannesburg 2196, South Africa

Penguin Books Ltd, Registered Offices: 80 Strand, London WC2R 0RL, England

First published by Penguin Group (Australia),
a division of Pearson Australia Group Pty Ltd, 2005

1 3 5 7 9 10 8 6 4 2

Designed by Miriam Rosenbloom © Penguin Group (Australia)
Series designed by David Altheim © Penguin Group (Australia)
Illustrations by Tom Jellett
Typeset in 13/21 pt Berkeley by Post Pre-press Group, Brisbane, Queensland
Printed in Australia by McPherson's Printing Group,
Maryborough, Victoria

National Library of Australia
Cataloguing-in-Publication data:

Moloney, James, 1954– .
68 teeth.
ISBN 0 14 330191 8.
1. Crocodiles – Juvenile fiction. I. Title.
(Series: Aussie chomps).
A823.3

www.puffin.com.au

CHAPTER 1

Jack Gordon was up early and dressed before his parents began to stir. It was the second day of the Christmas holidays and he'd spent all of the first one travelling the six hundred dusty kilometres home from his boarding school, All Souls St Gabriels, in Charters Towers. This morning he had woken up in his own bed on Long Mile Station, his family's cattle property in the Gulf Country, and he was going to celebrate his homecoming with a bit of fishing.

'Not yet, Minty,' he called to the dog dancing

excitedly around his legs. She was mostly boxer with a bit of cattle dog in her, though not enough to change the sandy brown colour of her coat. He swatted her playfully out of the way while he tied his rod and tackle box onto the side of his motorbike.

'There. All finished,' he said at last. He took his place in the saddle and gave Minty the command she'd been waiting for: 'Up.'

The dog immediately leapt into place behind him, digging her claws into the worn leather seat cover Jack's dad had attached for just that purpose. The warmth of Minty against his back made Jack think back to the night before when he'd arrived home and his parents had come out of the rambling homestead to meet him. Minty had been there with them, wagging her tail and barking, but he'd been expecting to see another dog as well.

'Where's Nutmeg?' he'd asked, looking around

for the pup they had kept from Minty's last litter. The pup would be almost fully grown by now, Jack had thought to himself on the long drive home, but there was no sign of him. One glance at his parents' solemn faces had warned him of bad news, even before his mother started to speak. 'He's run off, Jack. Or at least we haven't seen him for a week. We were hoping he'd turn up before you did. Probably chased something into the scrub and found a king brown instead. Dad looked for him the day after he went missing but . . .' She left the rest unsaid, finishing with a soft, 'I'm sorry.'

Jack was sorry too, but life could be pretty tough in the Gulf Country. Yet tough or not, it was where he belonged and it was where he liked to be. He planned to take over Long Mile from his father one day – it would be a big job, but it was a destiny he welcomed.

He kept an eye out for Nutmeg as he guided his bike across the paddocks towards the river. 'We'll probably find his bones under a tree one day,' he muttered into the wind that whipped at his face.

At barely fourteen, Jack wasn't old enough for a motorbike licence yet, but that didn't matter much on a cattle property. He'd been riding since he was nine – just a little Honda 125cc at first, but then on his twelfth birthday he'd graduated to the 250. It went like a rocket – once he was out of sight of the homestead, of course. The surrounding land was mostly flat and dry. To the uneducated eye, there wasn't much to see except for a few trees and the hardy bush grass that defied long seasons without rain. But Jack knew that riding across ground like that had its hazards. If you weren't careful, you could end up down the banks of a meandering river before you'd even seen it, especially travelling at eighty kilometres an hour. Luckily, Jack knew exactly where the river was.

But the rivers themselves could be strange beasts in the Gulf Country. In the wet season, they often became raging torrents that gouged their way through the sandy plains, the surging current cutting away a little more of the landscape each year. Jack knew there had been heavy rain just last month, though as he parked his bike above the steep bank it was hard for him to imagine just how deep and swollen this river must have been. The waters had receded weeks ago leaving a sedately flowing stream, just thirty metres across and no more than two or three metres deep.

Jack called to Minty, who was already sniffing and splashing in the muddy shallows. 'Get out of the water, you silly mongrel. You'll scare the fish.' Jack's voice was stern, but he was laughing as he threw a stick to her.

He was already thinking about the barramundi he hoped to catch that morning. Jack knew it was just about the best-tasting fish in Australia and that there were plenty to be caught in this river. No wonder he was happy to be home!

Climbing steadily in the sky, the sun was already hot on his skin. Nearby, three cattle made their cautious way down the high banks for a morning drink before the heat of the day. They looked at Jack with that 'Who are you?' look that only cattle seem to have. He ignored them and concentrated on adjusting the tension on his fishing line. Just as well, too, because moments later a fish struck. He yanked back on the line, jagging the hook firmly into the fish's mouth.

What a tug! 'It's a big barra for sure,' he called to Minty. He fought to bring the fish in, his rod bending almost double with the strain. 'This will feed the lot of us for a week!'

There was no great art to Jack's style of fishing. Reel it in and drag it out onto the bank was his usual way. But he did love the struggle! The rod jerked in his left hand as he wound in the line with his right. He had it into the shallows now. He watched as part of the barra's tail broke the surface before it dived again, determined to stay in the water.

Then *whoosh*! The line went slack. 'It must have spat out the hook,' he told Minty as he wound the reel. But there was something not quite right. A weight still dragged on the end of his line, not as heavy as before and definitely not alive, but something. He brought it to shore and lifted the end of the rod to raise his mysterious catch out of the water.

The head of a huge barramundi dangled from the hook. That was all – just the head. The body looked as if it had been cut away just behind the gills. Blood dripped down into the brown water.

'What happened to it?' Jack asked out loud. 'It's like something took a great huge bite –'

Before Jack could finish his sentence, he started shouting, 'Minty, away from the water!'

But dogs don't understand specific words, just the tone of their owner's voice. Minty was leaping around, only a metre from the water's edge, excited and half-frightened by the fear in Jack's cry. Jack had to lunge forward and grab at her collar. As soon as he had a firm grip, he began to drag his dog back up the bank.

Behind him, he heard a violent thrashing of water, and turning to look, he was just in time to see the strike. A huge crocodile shot out of the muddy water, fast as a cat and more powerful than a lion. Its terrible jaws snapped around the nearest leg it could find. A young steer let out a painful bellow. But worse was to come. The croc didn't hesitate for a second. It was already drawing back towards the water, dragging its desperate victim with it. The other cattle charged away in terror, not even stopping at the top of the high river bank to watch.

The crocodile now had their unfortunate companion all the way into the water. It flipped over suddenly, turning the steer with it. A sickening snap echoed across the mud and sand, and the steer bucked wildly in agony.

But the crocodile had only just begun. Still with that same grip, it flipped again and then began to spin over and over. The brown hide of the steer span with it. There was no more bellowing now. The steer's head remained under water most of the time. Every breath would fill its lungs with more water. It was losing the strength to fight back.

Still the croc turned over and over. Jack couldn't believe how big it was. It had to be at least four metres long. No, wait, the in-goal area on the school's footy field was five metres wide. It was that length, easily.

The muddy water around the two writhing animals was stained with another colour now, a rusty red. The water was foaming, and Jack noticed the bubbles had a pinkish tinge.

There was no hope for the steer. Half-drowned and rapidly losing blood, it was as good as dead. The croc sensed this as well. It stopped spinning the limp body around and slipped backwards into deeper water, taking the steer with it. If the poor animal wasn't already dead, it would drown soon enough.

The sudden silence after the fury of the attack came as a shock. Aside from the bubbles left behind by the wild thrashing, there was nothing to show of the deadly battle that had just been so easily won.

Jack watched, unable to move for many minutes, all the time holding onto Minty's collar so that she would not rush down to the water's edge. At last, he saw the crocodile again. It was well out into the deeper waters of the river now. It broke the surface and began to swim slowly towards the other side. In its massive jaws it held the headless carcass of the unlucky steer.

CHAPTER 2

Jack's fishing rod lay discarded on the soft sandy banks. With Minty's collar still firmly in his grasp, he struggled towards his bike. He reached it just as the shock of what he'd witnessed overwhelmed him. He began to shake, and perspiration oozed from every pore until his shirt was drenched.

Minty had been playing in the shallows, up to her knees. The croc could have taken her instead. And what about Jack himself? The croc had snapped at the barramundi right in front of him. Had it been watching him, waiting for the right moment to strike? He'd been standing only a rod's length from the water's edge. The croc had easily come out of the water that far to grab the steer. If it had come after him, Jack wouldn't have had a chance. It could have been his own headless body ploughing through the milky brown waters in the grip of those pitiless jaws.

Stop it, he told himself. There's no time for panic like this. I have to get back to the homestead to tell Dad.

He lifted Minty onto the pillion of his bike. The prospect of another ride calmed her down at last and prevented any more thoughts of racing back down to the river. Jack kicked the bike into life and headed back the way he'd come.

'You look like you've seen a ghost,' his mother joked when he fell into a chair beside the kitchen table. 'Now that you're back, I'll cook you breakfast just the way you like it.'

Jack ignored her offer. 'Where's Dad?' he asked anxiously.

'In the shed with Kelvin.'

Kelvin was the only other person who lived and worked on Long Mile. He'd known Jack's dad since their school days together.

'You'd better get them in here,' Jack said.

As soon as she heard the tone of his voice, Jack's mum stopped smiling. She went to the door and called once, loudly, the kind of summons no one ignores, and less than a minute later the two men entered the kitchen.

Jack was rapidly catching up to his father in height, but where he was still all elbows and long legs, his dad was well muscled from his work around the property. Jack's mum was always going on about how alike they were. Jack's dad didn't often say much, but Jack could usually tell what he was thinking just by looking at his eyes.

This morning, those eyes looked worried and tense.

When Jack told them what had happened at the river, his mother had to sit down at the table. 'It could have been you,' she whispered.

Jack's dad was more practical. 'It's the flooding from those rains last month. The crocs come upriver following the fish. The levels were higher than I've ever seen. That must be why one has come up this far. There hasn't been a croc in our river for twenty years.'

'Well, we've got one now and it's just taken a steer,' said Jack.

'Might not be the first one, either,' said Kelvin. He was a heavily built bushman – a 'front-row forward' Jack's dad liked to call him. The sun had turned his skin to deeply creased leather, especially his hands and the back of his neck. Unlike Jack's dad, Kelvin loved the chance to talk.

'That croc could have been in this part of the river for weeks. God knows what else it's taken.'

The kitchen fell silent as the three members of the Gordon family each realised what this might mean. It was left to Jack to say the name. 'Nutmeg.' He hadn't been bitten by a brown snake, as they'd suspected. What a horrible death, and the croc had nearly claimed Nutmeg's mother as well!

'What are we going to do?' Jack's mum asked.

'Shoot it,' said Jack immediately, the need to avenge poor Nutmeg heating his thoughts.

'Can't,' said Kelvin just as quickly. 'Crocodiles are a protected species these days.'

'But it's dangerous. Our cattle can't go near the river while it's there waiting for them.'

Jack's dad took charge. 'I'll get onto the Parks and Wildlife Service. They'll have to send someone up to trap it and take it back downstream,' he explained. 'In the meantime, fish is off the menu.

Don't go near the river until that big lizard's been caught.'

Jack didn't need to be told twice.

The trapper arrived two days later. Jack was expecting someone in neat khaki shorts and a shirt, like the guy he'd seen on TV back at boarding school. This guy wore filthy jeans and a blue singlet.

'Nils Fingleton,' he announced, sticking out a wiry hand for Jack's father to shake.

'Nils. Haven't heard that name before.'

'It's Norwegian. My grandfather was a Viking,' he said and then laughed at the look on their faces. 'Don't worry. The other side of my family has lived around the Gulf for a century. I used to shoot crocs for a living. Now I've got a licence to trap them.'

So he didn't work for the Parks and Wildlife

Service, Jack realised. They had just hired him and sent him out here to do the job for them. That would explain his truck. There were no government logos on the doors. In fact, the whole thing looked as if it had seen better days. Jack noticed it had a few special modifications, although the winch behind the driver's cabin didn't look as if it would be much good for dragging the truck out of a bog.

The trapper saw him staring at it. 'For hauling big crocs onto the tray,' he explained. 'I've caught some that weighed almost a tonne.'

'You'll need it for this one then. I saw it. It had to be at least five metres long.'

The trapper scoffed openly. 'Not likely this far upriver.'

Jack felt a bit insulted but he was intrigued by Nils Fingleton. He was a big bloke – a hundred and ninety centimetres tall, and thick around the middle. Like everyone who spent his life in the sun, Nils was deeply tanned. But unlike the crocodile heroes Jack had seen on the TV, Nils's hair wasn't blond. It was mostly grey like Jack's dad's, with just a bit of black to give it that salt-and-pepper look.

Nils shoved a battered bushman's hat onto his head and asked, 'Where did you see this monster, then?'

They showed him the river and Jack described what he'd seen.

'Sounds like a classic attack. Crocs can hear animals drinking at the water's edge, even when they're under water. Do you know what they call all that spinning round you saw?' he asked Jack, then answered himself without drawing breath. 'The death roll. On land it's not so lethal but not many survive once they're in the water. It's like a washing machine on spin cycle. The croc does it to disorient the victim, you see, so they don't know which way is up. Once the animal is drowned, it can't fight back any more.'

'Fight back,' Jack said. 'How can you fight back against something that strong?'

'Oh, crocs have their weak spots. One bloke up in New Guinea saved himself by poking a croc in the eye. The tips of their snouts are a bit sensitive, too. I saw a dog bite one on the nose once. Made him let go, I can tell you, but it didn't do the poor mongrel much good in the end. The croc came at him again and took his head off with a single snap.'

Nils used the thumb and forefinger of his left hand to demonstrate the action of a croc's jaws coming together. Jack noticed that Nils's thumb seemed a bit too short, but when he tried to look more closely, Nils kept his hand out of the way.

Nils had brought a tinnie with him – an

aluminium boat which he'd stowed upside down on the back of his truck. Jack and his dad helped Nils drag the boat down the steep bank. Once the powerful outboard motor was in place, he launched it into the lazy brown water.

'If it had a good feed a few days ago, it's probably basking in the sun somewhere along the bank. Shouldn't be too hard to spot.'

Jack looked at the boat. It seemed quite a bit shorter than the croc he had seen.

'Will you be safe?'

Nils just laughed. 'I know crocs and I respect 'em. Those two things have kept me alive this long.' He revved the outboard and took the little tinnie out into deeper water. 'I'll be back in an hour or two,' he called to them over his shoulder, and with a casual wave he disappeared around the bend.

*

Jack spent the rest of the afternoon helping his father fix fences. The pigs on their property had been at it again. A roo would just jump over a barbed wire fence and rabbits went under. But feral pigs – they'd go *through* a fence! Some of the big boars in the area were as high as a cattle dog at the shoulder. They were strong, too, and with hides too thick for barbed wire to penetrate, they had a habit of pushing against fences until they just snapped. Jack's dad was forever fixing Long Mile's fences.

They returned to the homestead to find Nils Fingleton's truck parked outside. He was in the kitchen, chatting away to Jack's mum.

'I saw it,' he called, as soon as Jack and his dad appeared in the doorway. 'A female saltie, about three metres long.'

He was watching Jack's face when he said this. Jack responded by raising his eyebrows in doubt.

Nils filled the kitchen with a hearty laugh. 'Don't worry, little mate, you're not the first person to overestimate the size of a croc. Especially when you've had a close call, like you did,' he said smugly.

Earlier Jack had felt insulted. Now he felt downright humiliated. 'That can't be right,' he protested. 'It had to be five metres, at least!' But who could argue with such experience? Nils had seen the culprit that had killed the steer and if he said it was no more than three metres, then that's how big it was.

They all sat down to dinner soon after. Nils couldn't hide his thumb now that he had to hold a fork. Jack had already been caught staring at it once so he held his tongue – but there was nothing to stop Kelvin.

'My thumb?' said the trapper when Kelvin asked him about it. 'Yep, it was a croc. A little one, it was. Took the tip right off. Lucky I didn't lose my whole hand.' He put down his fork and held the hand out for them all to see. 'There are six wounds on there, if you count them. Seventeen stiches in all.'

He didn't have to say it but Jack guessed there must be other old wounds scattered around his body. The frightening scene down at the river bank swam back into his memory. With an effort, he pushed it away. But he certainly didn't want to hear about any more of Nils's little accidents.

'How are you going to capture this croc?' he asked to change the topic.

'It's not too big to use a harpoon.'

'Wouldn't that kill it?'

'No, it's not the kind they use on whales. This harpoon just penetrates the skin deep enough to catch a hold. Then I can haul her in like a fish. Crocs get tired much faster than you'd expect. I could use a noose on its jaws too, I suppose.' Nils thought about what he'd said for a moment. 'No, come to think of it, I'd only try the harpoon or the noose if I had a couple of experienced blokes backing me up.'

'We'll help,' Jack's dad volunteered.

'No offence, but it's a risky business. It would have to be at night. How do you feel about jumping from a boat onto a croc's back – in the dark?'

Jack's father suddenly didn't seem so keen. Neither was Jack.

'Best to use the cylinder trap, I think,' said Nils, making up his mind. 'I'll set it up tomorrow.'

CHAPTER 3

The days start early on a cattle station. Nils Fingleton was a bushie like the rest of them at Long Mile and was already checking his equipment when Jack came out of the kitchen the next morning to let Minty off her lead.

‘Where will you set the trap?’ he asked Nils.

‘I saw the perfect place yesterday while I was out looking for the croc. It’s about five or six kilometres up from where I put the boat in. I should be able to get close enough with the truck and then carry what I need from there. Say, you can't drive can you?'

'Yeah, a motorbike,' Jack told him proudly.

'No, I was thinking about the truck. I have to get the tinnie upriver as well, from where I left it.'

Jack suspected the trapper might be making fun of him again. 'I've only just turned fourteen, but I did have a bit of a go at driving once on an old bomb Dad keeps around the place.' Jack chose not to mention to Nils the fact that he'd made a complete mess of it. He'd kangaroo-jumped the old car nonstop until finally his father had said, 'Better stick to the bikes until you're a bit older.'

Jack *was* able to help out though. He hopped on his motorbike and followed Nils's truck to a spot close to the river where the trap was going to be set. Then he gave Nils a ride on the pillion of his bike, following the river from the high ground until they stopped above the tinnie which the trapper had pulled well out of the water the afternoon before. Jack was forced to hold Minty across his thighs during the trip so it was all a bit cramped.

Once they arrived, Jack had to grab the dog's collar to stop her quenching her thirst down at the river's edge. Until that croc was caught, all drinks would have to come from a tap.

Nils took his boat upstream, then drove back to the homestead later in the day to eat with the family.

'I'll sleep in my truck tonight,' he told them. 'I have to know if the croc takes the bait. They can do themselves a lot of damage in a trap. If the trap rolls back into the water, the poor thing will drown.'

Poor thing? thought Jack.

'Can I stay out there with you?' he asked.

Nils looked surprised but didn't refuse straight

away. He liked to talk – that much was pretty obvious. Perhaps he liked the idea of having an audience for the evening.

But Jack's mum and dad soon killed off their son's hopes. 'No chance. You're staying safe in your bed. That croc has nearly had you once already and we're not going to give it a second chance.'

'But I'd just be watching for the croc with Mr Fingleton.'

Nils put him right on that score. 'Sorry, little mate. I'll probably take a look around in the tinnie as well, using a spotlight. Crocs are active at night. It's their favourite feeding time.'

Nothing happened on that first night. But Nils didn't seem too worried when Jack rode into his camp the next morning.

'They're clever things, crocs,' he said. 'Been

around for sixty-five million years so I suppose they've learned a thing or two. She might have come around for a bit of a look last night. Could take a few nights for her to get inquisitive. She'll be hungry again by then. Come on, I'll show you the trap.'

He led Jack through the low bushes that screened his truck from the river. It wasn't far – fifty metres maybe. As soon as they reached the top of the bank, Jack could see the trap. A cylinder, Nils had called it, and that was a fair description. It was about a metre and a half in diameter and at least six metres long. The sides were made of stout chain wire laid over steel hoops, which gave the trap its shape.

The bottom lip of the open end was submerged a little way into the river. At the far end, the chunk of meat Jack's dad had provided as bait was suspended on some wires. Jack scanned the wires and saw how they would trigger the gate to close over the open end of the trap if the meat were disturbed. It was hard to see because there were so many other ropes and wires stretching out from the cylinder. Each one was attached to a heavy peg hammered into the ground and pulled very tight.

'These keep the trap in place when the croc starts complaining,' Nils said, touching one of the ropes. 'Once she works out she's trapped, she won't be too happy. She'll roll and thrash about but it won't do her any good. When she's exhausted, I'll get a tranquilliser into her and winch her onto the truck.'

When Jack got back to the homestead later that morning his dad had a proposition for him. 'Kelvin and I are going to check the boundary fences. Should take two days and there's no point coming back here halfway through. We'll camp in the open. Do you want to come?'

Jack loved sleeping under the stars and normally he would have jumped at his dad's offer. Not this time though.

'It's that croc, isn't it?' his father said with a grin.

'I really want to see it,' Jack confessed. 'If Mr Fingleton catches it tonight, he'll have it onto the back of his truck and gone before we get back.'

So Jack stayed, keeping his mum company in the house. That night Nils stayed out by the trap and cooked his own dinner.

The next morning, Jack took Minty on his bike to scout the river on his own. He knew he would be safe as long as he stayed high on the banks. Nils never seemed to stop telling him about a crocodile's habits and one of the things he'd said was: 'Crocs don't like going more than a couple of body lengths from water. And they won't climb a steep bank either, unless some drongo from the city has left a pile of stinking fish carcasses behind after a fishing trip.'

Jack ventured a little way downstream from where he'd seen the croc attack and then stopped suddenly. At the water's edge just below him he could see a tinnie beached awkwardly. It had to be Nils's. He called the man's name but wasn't surprised when there was no reply. No bushman would leave a boat in that position on purpose. It must have drifted to this spot and found the shore by accident.

It was an effort to keep the worst images from running through his mind. Nils had talked about spotlighting at night to see if the croc was around. Had he gone out in the boat again last night? If he had, why was it here now, abandoned?

Jack stopped himself from thinking any further

along those lines. But it wasn't easy to deny the possibilities. The croc might have rammed the boat. If Nils was standing up, he could have fallen overboard. Jack could hear the splash in his mind. Once in the water, the guy wouldn't stand a chance.

The image of a human body being pushed sideways through the water, propelled by the awesome power of a huge crocodile, tormented him.

'We'd better go look for him,' Jack said to Minty. He watched the water carefully for a few minutes. Not that this achieved much. 'Minty, here,' he called and when the dog came to him, he picked her up. He took five hurried strides and tossed Minty into the boat. In one quick movement, he shoved the boat free of the mud and levered himself over the side, landing in an untidy pile of arms and legs in the bottom.

The outboard motor started first time and,

with his eyes scouring the water's surface, Jack manoeuvred the tinnie out of the shallows. Then he revved up the power and turned to head upstream, towards Nils's truck and the cylinder trap.

Jack wasn't sure if he really wanted to arrive. If there was no sign of Nils near the trap or back at his truck, there could only be one conclusion. It was too horrible to think about.

The river twisted and turned through the flat country. Along every inch of the way, Jack's eyes darted from the water's surface ahead to the left bank, then the right. What he'd do if he actually saw the croc swimming towards him, he had no idea. It seemed like the longest boat ride he'd ever taken.

At last he rounded a bend and there was the trap. Better yet, there was Nils himself, on the river bank beside it. The croc hadn't taken him after all. Relief flooded through Jack's body. He aimed the tinnie into the shore, beaching it about forty metres short of the trap. Nils came to meet him.

'You found my boat, I see. Thanks for bringing it back.'

'How did it get downstream?'

'My own stupid fault,' Nils confessed. 'I was in such a hurry to leave it last night that I didn't pull it up the beach properly. I couldn't follow it in the dark but I knew it wouldn't drift too far. Besides, I had other business to attend to.'

His face broke into a huge grin and with the flourish of an actor on stage, he turned and swept his arm towards the trap. Jack had been too busy with the boat to even notice the trap until now. At this invitation from Nils he turned to look. Resting quietly in the centre of the metal cylinder was a three-metre crocodile.

CHAPTER 4

'She turned up while I was out in the tinnie,' Nils said. 'Come on, you probably want a closer look.'

Yes, thought Jack, but how close! 'She can't get out, can she?' Jack asked, before he could stop himself.

'No, it's perfectly safe. She's already had a good thrash around so she's exhausted.'

Exhausted or not, the croc opened its jaws and hissed when Jack approached. 'If you ever hear that sound down near a river bank, back away towards dry land quick smart. That's the sound of one angry crocodile.'

Jack stopped four metres short of the trap. This was as near as he needed to get, he decided, even if Nils did say it was completely safe. He was surprised by the dabs of yellow and grey that stood out along the side of the croc's head. He hadn't remembered that. His memory from the other day was of a dark fiend, mostly black and thundercloud grey, but then the violence of the attack hadn't left him much chance to judge the croc's colour.

Nils had been right about the length. The croc would barely measure three metres from her nose to the tip of her tail. Jack was forced to admit that in his own terror he must have exaggerated the animal's size.

He felt Minty brush against his leg. Her hackles were raised. Every muscle in her body was tensed and she let out a low, challenging snarl.

'Stop it,' Jack ordered, but it was too late. Without warning, the croc jerked inside the cylinder, its whole body writhing from side to side while its jaws gnashed at the air. Both Jack and Minty got a huge fright and jumped away together. Jack halted after a stagger or two but not Minty. She scooted ten metres along the bank before she turned around again. Even then, she looked ready to go another ten, or maybe a hundred.

'Little coward,' laughed Nils, watching the dog.

That was a bit unfair, thought Jack. 'I've seen her take on a black snake. She killed it, too.'

'Yeah, all right. I suppose a croc like this is more than you could expect her to stand up to,' said Nils, backing down a little.

Jack retraced the few steps he had retreated, ready for any sudden movements and determined to stand his ground. 'Where will you take her?'

'Down the coast somewhere. If it were a male, he'd have to fight for a bit of territory, but this one shouldn't have much trouble relocating. She's a good specimen. Her teeth look fine.'

'Yeah, beautiful,' Jack answered in a grim voice.

'I'm serious. Crocs are a bit like humans, you see. If they're missing a few teeth, it's a sign they're getting old.' He moved to stand only a metre from the chain wire in front of the croc's head. The big reptile opened its mouth obligingly, like a patient at the dentist. 'This one's still got the lot, by the look of it. Sixty-eight teeth. Count them if you like.'

'No, thanks. I've seen what they can do.'

'Fascinating creatures, though, don't you think? The perfect killing machine. Salties like this have been known to take on sharks out in the ocean.'

'If it's a saltwater croc, what's it doing two hundred kilometres from the sea?' Jack asked.

Nils walked slowly along the length of the trapped reptile, admiring every centimetre. 'Just a name. Freshwater crocs have to stay in the rivers because salt is no good for them. But this kind, with the rounded snout, they can live anywhere. That one there might never taste salt water in her whole lifetime.' Nils nodded towards the trap and then turned and made the return journey to the croc's head.

'They go wherever there's food. Trouble is they get stranded when the water level drops. Look at those eyelids. Aren't they a marvel of evolution?' He coaxed Jack closer, bending over himself to get a better look. 'You can't see it but she's got three eyelids and one of them is see-through. That way, she can see just as well under water as above it.'

'Sounds a bit like wearing goggles in a swimming pool,' said Jack, beginning to show some interest.

But Nils had finished his biology lesson. He followed the cylinder trap all the way to the water's edge, checking on the gate that stopped the croc from backing into the river. 'This job has gone better than I'd hoped. They pay me to catch the croc but the money's the same no matter how long it takes. To catch this one in two nights is a bonus. I could have been out here all week.'

Jack trailed after Nils to the muddy shore, but even though the crocodile was there in the trap, plain for him to see, something made him keep his boots dry. Nils didn't seem to have the same concerns. His boots splashed lightly in the water as he rattled the sturdy gate with his hand. 'Nothing's going to break through that,' he muttered. 'Come on. Time to get this croc onto my truck.'

He pointed to the lip of the steep river bank where he had already brought the truck earlier, reversing it into place so that the tray faced towards the river.

Nils started up the bank. He had come about five paces away from the water when it suddenly erupted behind him as though the river itself had burped violently. But it wasn't foul air that came rushing out. Before Nils had even heard the disturbance, he started bellowing in agony. His left foot had disappeared inside the jaws of a huge crocodile which had taken hold of him to halfway up his calf.

The crocodile was almost a full body length out of the water. Now, with a solid hold on its prey, it was already backing away into the river, dragging Nils with it.

'No!' he cried, desperately hooking his fingers into the chain wire of the trap and pulling with all his might. Jack couldn't stand to see the pain on his face.

Yet still Jack hadn't moved. The attack had come so quickly that it took him a few moments to register what had happened. Then he came to life. He couldn't let Nils be dragged into the water. That was the croc's home turf. Nils wouldn't stand a chance once the croc began that terrifying death roll. Nils had said as much himself.

Jack bent down quickly, grabbed two fistfuls of Nils's shirt and began to tug him backwards. But he soon realised that the shirt was simply pulling over the man's head. He reached forward again and took hold of Nils's belt instead.

The croc was incredibly strong. Even with Nils's steely hands locked onto the chain wire and Jack doing what he could, it jerked its human victim viciously. It would surely bite Nils's leg off. Then Nils's grip on the trap was broken and he was yanked a metre closer to the water. Bravely, he somehow managed to grab hold of the trap again, but the damage those teeth were doing to his leg was horrible.

Nils couldn't hold on much longer. Only his will to survive had kept him on the muddy bank this long. Jack had to do something. Tugging against the crocodile's overwhelming strength was useless. Where his next idea came from, he didn't really know. Perhaps it was all the information that had streamed out of Nils's mouth – everything anyone would ever want to know about crocodiles. Whatever the source, Jack suddenly let go of Nils's belt, took two strides towards the croc and punched it hard, right on the tip of its snout.

His fist exploded in pain. He wasn't a fighter – he'd never punched anyone before in his life. If it hurts like this, he thought to himself, he never would. It felt as though every bone in his hand was broken.

But the crocodile let go of Nils's leg. And then it backed away into the river and disappeared beneath the surface.

Nils was flat on his back, moaning and clutching at his leg. Jack took one look at it and had to turn away. Everything was still there, the boot and his left leg emerging from the sock, but the lower part of his calf was a mess. Pale pink flesh gaped through the many gashes in the skin. And that dull whiteness he could see in the deepest cuts was . . . yes, it had to be bone. Blood was everywhere.

Jack thought he might be sick but fought hard to resist. Nils was doing his best to crawl backwards along the side of the cylinder trap. Jack had to help him.

'To the highest ground,' Nils gasped. At the

same time, he was using his good leg and his arms to keep moving. But after only a body length, he was exhausted and the shock of his injuries gave way to pain, leaving him faint.

Jack shook him awake and together they managed to travel another body length before Nils collapsed again. He raised himself onto his elbows and looked back towards the river. His gasp made Jack's head snap round. The crocodile had surfaced again, the top half of its body clearly visible from nose to tail.

'It will come after me again. The smell of blood is too strong,' groaned Nils. 'Get yourself up the bank. Hurry, before it grabs you instead.'

He tried to push Jack away towards safety but Jack wouldn't go. He tugged at Nils's belt again, making no progress at all.

'That bit of wood there,' cried Nils. His arm flopped beside his body as he tried to point. Jack looked around and saw the branch of a gum tree that had been drifting in the river. The receding waters had left it stranded in the mud. He rushed to fetch it, snapping off the thinner end until he was holding a sturdy club about the size of a baseball bat.

'Bring it here,' Nils demanded.

Jack wondered if Nils seriously thought he could beat away that monster with just a stick. Surely before he could swing the club that croc would have his whole body between its jaws.

'Give it to me!' Nils roared when Jack hesitated.

But there was no time to argue. The crocodile was on the move again. There was no lightning surge from the water's edge this time. It came on cautiously, emitting a low rumble from deep in its throat. No punch from Jack could save Nils now. Jack would surely lose his arm if he even attempted it. The only weapon they had between them was the lump of driftwood in Jack's hands.

'Get up the bank,' Nils cried. At the sight of the crocodile's approach he made another frenzied attempt to slither out of range, but the effort was too much. He flopped back in the mud and sand, groaning like a man who knew death had come for him.

The crocodile edged forward. Now a new sound broke the eerie deathwatch on the river bank. It was Minty. She dashed between Jack and the crocodile, barking like a machine gun.

'Get away, you stupid mongrel,' Jack shouted at her.

The croc hesitated for a second, sizing up the dog, then lunged at her, its jaws snapping only centimetres from her shoulder. Minty leapt away just in time, but didn't bolt as she had when the smaller reptile had writhed in her cage. Minty seemed more terrified even than Jack, but would defend her master no matter how great the danger.

If Jack wanted to save her, he would have to keep the croc off balance. With the creature distracted by Minty's frenzied dancing, he dared two quick paces and smashed the shortened tree branch against the croc's sensitive snout.

The creature turned towards him immediately, but Jack had been careful to stay well balanced and, as soon as the blow landed, he bounded backwards five, six, seven rapid steps until he saw that the croc was not coming after him.

It was still after the crazy dog, though. Jack rushed in again and slammed the driftwood onto the same spot. The croc lunged at him this time, but he had stayed on the balls of his feet and sprang away almost as soon as contact was made. The croc opened its massive jaws and Jack expected to hear a roar, like an angry lion.

Instead, that ominous hiss warned him of the creature's fury.

Minty was becoming more ferocious too – and more reckless. She darted in, drawing the croc's attention to herself, barking at every breath. One miscalculation and those jaws would snatch the body clean off the top of her legs.

The same applied to Jack. If he slipped in the treacherous mud, he would surely be snapped in half. Did he dare another attack? He gulped down a breath and came at the monster again, but with a demented dog on one side and a boy wielding a vicious club on the other, the croc retreated to the comfort of the water again. It did not submerge this time but stayed watching, like a log with eyes, waiting for its confusion to clear and eager to taste more blood.

Chapter 5

Nils had called out many times during Jack's fight with the croc, but Jack had steadily ignored him. With great courage and determination Nils had managed to drag himself further from the river. He was well beyond the end of the cylinder trap now, fifteen metres from the river's edge. That was as far as he was likely to get though. The bank became much steeper at this point.

The effort of crawling had taken the last of Nils's strength so that when Jack reached him, he was slipping in and out of consciousness. He was speaking but none of the words made sense.

Jack made himself look at the wounded leg. No wonder Nils was barely conscious. A trail of blood marked his path along the side of the trap. He was still losing blood at an alarming rate – rich red blood. Jack knew what this meant. The croc's teeth had punctured an artery inside the leg. If he couldn't stop the bleeding quickly then it wouldn't be the croc that finished off poor Nils.

He looked towards the water. Death still stalked them but, for now, it was biding its time.

What should I do? Jack thought. Then he remembered. He had just done a surf lifesaving course. What a joke! He lived two hundred kilometres from the Gulf. His school in Charters Towers was just as far from the Pacific Ocean, but they had organised a course. And the instructor had shown them how to apply a tourniquet.

He began to unbutton his shirt. When his

fingers fumbled on the last button, he simply yanked if off. Then he ripped it into strips and knotted one around Nils's leg, just below the knee. He held the strip firm, slipped a small stick into place and then wound the homemade bandage round and round until Nils groaned in his semiconsciousness. But Jack could see that the bleeding had slowed.

Renewed barking from Minty warned him that the croc was stirring. He had to get Nils over the lip of the river bank – and quickly. With a glance at the tourniquet to make sure it was still tight, he moved around behind Nils. He slipped his hand under the man's armpits and pulled.

It was hopeless. The guy was simply too big and heavy and the bank was getting too steep. Jack huffed and heaved for half a minute and moved Nils ten centimetres at most. He needed help.

His motorbike was back down the river where

he'd first spotted the boat. To reach the homestead on foot would take an hour and by the time they had returned, there wouldn't be any Nils left to save. He simply couldn't leave the poor man alone. Frantically, Jack looked around him. The trap. If he released the smaller croc and both he and Nils crawled inside . . .

But, no, who was he kidding – then he would have two crocs on the loose. He couldn't even move Nils anyway, how would he get him inside the 'safety' of the cylinder trap?

Jack needed to think of another plan. There was the truck, but it was up there beyond the steep banks. He could roll it down the bank and get Nils inside it somehow. But then he'd still have the same problem as before – Nils was too heavy for him to budge.

Wait! The reason the truck was there was to collect the female already inside the trap. That croc must weigh half a tonne, much more than Nils. Nils was going to get the croc onto the tray of his truck using the winch. That was it! The winch.

Jack raced up the bank and to the door of the truck. He knew about winches. His father had shown him. This one needed the engine's power to make it work. 'Please let the keys be in the ignition,' he prayed. Jack wrenched open the cabin door and breathed a sigh of relief when he spied the keys. Twisting them clockwise he heard the truck's engine crank into life. Moments later he was on the back of the truck, inspecting the winch. Yes, there was the lever that engaged the engine. He pulled it towards him and saw the barrel of the winch begin to turn. Wrong way! He shoved the lever impatiently in the opposite direction. The winch complained with a rasping and clattering of gears.

Then the barrel stopped. Jack thought his own heart had stopped along with it. Had he wrecked the thing before he could use it? Suddenly, the barrel began to turn again, the right way this time. The finger-thick wire was unwinding.

'Harness – I'll need some kind of harness,' Jack reminded himself.

He found what he needed in a box to the side of the tray. Then, grabbing the end of the wire, he hurried back towards the river. Or at least, he tried to hurry. How slowly was the winch turning? The next two minutes were agony. Jack needed thirty metres of slack before he could reach Nils. He had never walked thirty metres so slowly in his life.

What he saw when he reached the lip of the steep river bank didn't help his peace of mind. The crocodile had come out of the water after Minty. The dog snarled and jigged about bravely, but the beast was still advancing, taking a small step towards Nils every few seconds.

Finally Jack reached Nils's now unconscious body. He slipped the harness over Nils's shoulders, one arm at a time, until it was secure across his chest and under his armpits. The wire was attached to a strap behind his neck. It was ready to go.

Minty's loud barking caused Jack to look up sharply. The croc was closer now. But only the winch could move Nils. Jack shot up the bank to the truck. The engine was still idling, thank God. If it stalled now, Nils was finished. A tug on the lever, towards himself this time, produced the same grinding sounds as before, but the winch finally started turning in the opposite direction. By the time it became taut, Jack was already on the move, hurtling towards Nils's slumped figure. He reached him just as Nils was jerked backwards for the first time.

Poor guy, Jack thought, watching as Nils's shoulders dug into the soft soil beneath them. Jack grabbed Nils's shirt and tried to lift him, to help him slip over the ground as easily as possible. But then he realised that he hadn't checked the position of the croc for a while. He turned his head and let out a yell. The crocodile was only three metres away!

The club! Where was that piece of driftwood he had used before?

It was no use. Jack remembered that he'd foolishly dropped the club towards the water. If the croc attacked now, there was nothing he could do to defend himself. And if he backed away, it would go for Nils. The winch was steadily pulling Nils towards safety, but what was the point if the crocodile mauled him horribly before he reached the top of the bank?

Jack leapt to the side. The croc turned towards

him a little, suspicious of the sudden movement. Jack leapt in front of it again and then to the other side. The croc snapped its jaws and followed his dance, but came no closer to Nils. And all the while, the winch did its desperately slow work.

Minty worried at the croc from behind. It didn't like being attacked from two sides at once, no matter how defenceless the attackers were. It lashed its tail at Minty. She wasn't fast enough this time and the tail caught her, just a glancing blow but enough to make her unsteady on her feet for a second. The croc swivelled around towards her. Jack could hardly believe a beast this size could move so fast and with such agility. It lunged at Minty and a frightened yelp immediately echoed around the shore.

'Minty!' Jack cried, fearing the worst. But Minty had scampered away before the croc could come at her a second time. Blood trickled from a wound high on her foreleg. If she had been a few centimetres closer, those teeth would have caught her in their terrible vice.

It was all becoming too much for the hungry croc. The game of stealth was now over. Its victim was slowly disappearing up the bank. It turned back, smelling the trail of blood that still leaked from Nils's damaged leg. The croc advanced towards him and there was nothing Jack or Minty could do this time to stop it. On it came, slowed a little by the steepening bank but still set on its course.

It drew level with the female still marooned inside the cylinder trap. The presence of such an enormous body nearby unnerved the captured croc. She hissed and began to thrash about wildly inside the wire. The male turned towards her and snapped his jaws, as though warning her off. But this only made the violent shuddering inside the cage get worse. The two creatures were setting each other off now. Protective wire lay between them but this didn't seem to matter – they might as well have been out on some mud bank somewhere, threatening each other.

And all the while, the winch kept up its slow, slow work, pulling the unconscious Nils towards the top of the river bank.

Jack stayed by Nils, lifting his head and shoulders as best he could to ease the journey. With the crocodile distracted, Jack began to hope. Maybe they would make it after all. The lip of the river bank was only a few metres away. Surely if Jack could just get Nils over the top, they would be safe. Finally they reached the edge of the bank. Nils's limp body bent awkwardly as the angle of the wire changed. He was being dragged over dusty grass now instead of sand. What now? Jack wondered. He had brought Nils this far but he couldn't just leave him there on the ground.

There was only one solution. Jack had seen two wooden planks in the back of Nils's truck. He guessed they must be what Nils used as a ramp to get his huge captives onto the tray. One would surely be enough for a human being. Jack grabbed a plank and noticed how the surface had been brushed smooth by the countless heavy bodies that had been dragged across it. It was just as well, or else Nils would have ended up with a back full of splinters.

With the plank in place, Jack guided Nils towards its lower end as the winch ground on. He eased Nils's shoulders onto the plank and then jumped onto the tray and waited for the winch to do its work. In less than a minute, Nils would be aboard the truck and safe from the croc at last.

Or would he? A renewed round of barking from Minty made Jack look up. To his horror, he saw that the croc had breached the lip of the river bank and now lay on the grass, watching. The sight of the truck and the workings of the winch were beyond its understanding, but it knew one thing – its prey was escaping. Suddenly, it shot across the flat ground, its tail sweeping from side to side, its short legs working frantically as it powered towards the ramp.

Nils's head, shoulders and torso were already on the tray of the truck. Jack had to take the risk. In the face of the on-rushing croc, he pulled the ramp out from under Nils and let it drop to the ground.

The croc couldn't slither up the ramp and maul them now, but Nils's legs still dangled over the edge. The croc could see them. It was readying itself to lunge upwards. Jack hooked his arms under Nils's armpits and, finding strength he didn't realise he possessed, wrenched the man's body backwards.

Jack lost balance in the effort and almost ended up underneath Nils as the winch continued to drag them towards the cabin. Then he scrambled free and reached for the lever to stop the winch turning. He could see the jaws of the croc in brief snatches as it arched back and lunged upwards. It was all in vain now. Nils was safe.

CHAPTER 6

Minty was still on the ground beside the truck but was too wary of the croc to let herself be caught again. In fact, now that her master was safe, she had retreated a sensible distance and stood watching the croc, snarling, with her front legs poised to attack and her rear legs ready to flee.

Jack looked down at Nils. Poor guy. His eyes were twitching as he fought to regain consciousness. The pain in his leg must be awful, but it was the blood Jack was more worried about. Nils had lost so much. Jack had to get him back to the homestead.

But how? The homestead was six kilometres away. Even with his bike, it would have been impossible to ride with Nils in the state he was in. Jack felt the steady purr of the truck's engine. If only his dad had been more patient and let him have another go on that old car.

But wait a minute. Jack *had* made a mess of his first driving lesson, but at least he knew which pedals to push. He also knew what a clutch did and how to work the gearstick and the accelerator. Maybe he could . . .

The driver's door was still open from when he'd started the engine earlier. Jack swung round from the tray and hopped into the seat, making sure he stayed off the ground. Okay, there were the pedals. He could just reach them. He pushed in the clutch with his left foot and took hold of the gearstick. He had to find first gear. It was to the left and forward in a car. He tried the same movements. There was a terrible clashing of gears then a 'thunk'. It wasn't the best way to do it, but at least the truck was in gear. Now for the clutch. This was where he'd made such a fool of himself in that old bomb. He pressed down on the accelerator with his right foot. The engine roared way too loudly but he didn't even hear it. His mind was focused entirely on his left foot. Slowly, Jack told himself, let the clutch out slowly. This was worse than waiting for the winch. At last he could feel the truck inching forward. He let the clutch out a little more, a little faster. Suddenly the whole vehicle lurched forward and the engine died.

Damn! He'd stalled it. He slammed his foot down on the clutch and turned the key. The engine began to purr again and then roar violently as Jack pressed the accelerator. He let out the clutch, but this time when the truck began to move, he didn't panic. Slowly, he thought, still slowly. The truck began to buck reluctantly again but Jack didn't take his foot off the clutch and the engine stayed alive. He was rolling forward, a little jerkily, but he kept his foot steady on the accelerator and the bucking subsided. At last he'd got the truck moving.

Time to change gear. Jack pushed in the clutch again and yanked the gearstick backwards. The clunking and clashing of metal against metal was even worse than before but at least he'd found second gear. When he let his foot off the clutch, the jerking stopped altogether. He was rolling along at twenty kilometres an hour and all he had to do was keep going.

Jack heard the sound of barking and looked out his window to see Minty running alongside the truck. He flung open the door and called out to her. With a single bound she leapt into the truck and Jack caught hold of her collar. Her legs scratched feverishly across Jack's thighs and he pushed her onto the passenger seat beside him.

Now it was time to concentrate on driving. He could not afford to stop in case he couldn't get going again. The ground was open and flat, with not a tree to crash into, thankfully, but he needed a road so that he didn't get lost, or worse, get bogged in an unseen hole. He steered the truck away from the river and breathed a sigh of relief when he spotted a dirt track worn down by three generations of his family as they travelled around Long Mile.

Jack turned onto the track and headed for the homestead. He even worked up the courage to change gear again – to third this time – pushing forward into neutral, across towards himself and then forward again. There was no gut-wrenching 'thunk' this time. Hey, he could do this!

Then he saw the gate up ahead. How could he have forgotten about the gate? There was only one fence between this part of the property and the homestead, but there it was, a hundred metres ahead of him, and coming closer with every second.

Always close the gate. It was the first rule bush kids learned as they were growing up. That day, Jack broke the rule. In fact, he broke the gate as well. With only fifty metres left to go, he made up his mind. Nils's truck had a heavy bullbar across the front. The gate was held in place by a chain looped over an L-shaped catch screwed into the hardwood post. He was pretty sure which would win out in a battle between the two.

'Hold tight,' he called to Minty. He gripped the steering wheel and pressed his foot down flat on the accelerator. By the time the truck hit the gate, they were travelling at seventy kilometres an hour. The gate was blasted right off its hinges.

Jack ducked behind the wheel at the last second in case a piece of broken gate smashed through the windscreen. Looking up again quickly, he could see the cluster of buildings that formed the homestead no more than a kilometre away.

He gunned the engine once more, desperate now to cover the remaining distance as quickly as possible. Nils's life depended on it, or at least Jack hoped it did. He had no way of knowing whether Nils was still alive and was hardly about to stop the truck to find out, not when he was so close to help. With hundreds of metres still to go, Jack leaned on the horn to warn his mother, but then clutched the wheel in both hands again, determined to guide the truck through the space between the shed and the end of the house as best he could.

There, he was through, and there was his

mother, waiting on the verandah outside the kitchen, her hand to her mouth when she saw who was at the wheel. Time to stop, Jack realised. He stamped hard on the brake and the truck slowed immediately, but as he tried to bring it to a halt near his mother, the vehicle bucked and shuddered wildly. The clutch! Jack had forgotten all about it. With a final lurch, the engine stalled and the desperate journey was over.

But there was no time to rest. Jack jumped out of the cab and called to his astonished mother, 'Nils is hurt. A croc has ripped his leg open.' He pointed towards the bed of the truck where Nils lay unconscious.

Shocked though she was, Jack's mother had known many emergencies in her time on Long Mile. As Jack looked on, she examined Nils's ravaged leg without flinching, then lifted Nils's arm and pressed her fingertips to his wrist.

'He's still alive and his pulse is strong. We'd better call the flying doctor,' she said, leaving her son to shade Nils from the sun as she hurried inside to the two-way radio.

'They're on their way,' she assured Jack, when she returned a few minutes later with the homestead's medical kit. 'We have to keep him warm and make sure he doesn't lose any more blood.'

She took a specially made tourniquet from the medical kit, but when she went to release the makeshift one Jack had created, she stopped. 'I think it's already doing the job as well as it can,' she decided and left it in place. 'Thank God you stopped the loss of blood, Jack. He would have bled to death by now if you hadn't.'

She glanced around at the truck which had brought Nils from the river and the harness of the winch still looped under Nils's armpits and realised that her son had done more than just apply a bushman's tourniquet. Then she looked up at Jack's face, exhausted by his recent ordeal, and saw a young man staring down at her.

'It's all right, Jack,' she whispered. 'He'll make it.'

EPILOGUE

Nils Fingleton still traps crocodiles for a living. He's quite famous around the Gulf Country these days. After all, not many people suffer an attack like he did and live to tell the tale. He limps a little, favouring his left leg, but he still has both legs to walk on. He tells anyone who cares to listen that he owes his left leg, and his life as well, to a young man named Jack Gordon, from out there at Long Mile Station.

Of course, Nils had more than just Jack to thank for his recovery. There was the flying doctor who arrived on the plane from Mount Isa and the surgeon in Cairns who operated on his leg. But those details tend to be forgotten.

'Jack was the one,' Nils would say. 'All those doctors and nurses couldn't have done a thing for me if Jack hadn't fought off that croc. More than five metres long, it was, and the boy scared it off with a punch on the nose!'

He carries a photo of the croc with him in his wallet.

Two days after the attack, a team of trappers went out to Long Mile to remove the female from the cylinder trap. They left the trap in place and six days later it was full again, with the croc that had attacked Nils. The plan was to relocate it down on the coast, three hundred kilometres from the nearest town.

Jack didn't go down to see the croc before it left.

'I've been close enough to count its teeth,' he told his parents and then added under his breath, 'all sixty-eight of them!'

About James Moloney

James was born in Sydney in 1954, which makes him pretty old. He lives in Brisbane these days with his long-suffering wife and three children. They think he's 'orright' and one of them lists him as her third-favourite author.

In 1977 James drove around Queensland's Gulf Country with some friends. The weather was sweltering and because they were a hundred kilometres from the sea they thought it was safe to swim, only to hear a man shouting at them, 'Get out of the water! There might be crocs!'

That trip helped James describe the countryside for this story.

Over the years he's collected odd bits of information about crocodiles and crocodile attacks. Many of these facts found their way into *68 Teeth* and helped make it as authentic and scary as possible. James has mentioned All Souls St Gabriels School in the story because he went there once to meet the students and many of them come from around the Gulf of Carpentaria. Hi guys!

www.puffin.com.au

Every full moon Walter's family turned into handsome werewolves, but Walter was different.

Grommet lives life on the edge.

Tony's dad wants Tony to be a footy superstar.

Can Pete and Morris conquer the ten metre diving tower? It's a matter of life, death, love and discount icy poles!